Watson

And the Terrific Ten

J.H. Willard Publishing
Books with Character

Adela

Merry Christmas!

John Eric Johnson

Watson

And the Terrific Ten

By John Eric Johnson
Illustrations by Isabel Arribas

JEJ Wizard Publishing
Books with Character

Copyright

First Printing, 2020

ISBN 978-1-7343553-7-6 (Print)

ISBN 978-1-7343553-8-3 (eBook)

JEBWizard Publishing

37 Park Forest Rd,

Cranston, RI 02920

www.jebwizardpublishing.com

JEBWizard Publishing
Books with Character

Dedication

To Georgia Lyles, who when asked who her favorite reindeer was giggled and said "Watson." From that one word came the story that follows. Thank you Gee!

Table of Contents

Chapter I Beginning or the End

Her little nose pressed up against the frost-covered window, Georgia shivered as icy-cold air crept into her room like an uninvited guest. The wind howled. The windows and shutters banged and clattered — like the drums and cymbals Santa was placing this very night under Christmas trees.

Georgia was worried.

One of the worst snowstorms to hit the North Pole in the past 100 years was raging outside, and Santa Claus and his reindeer were long overdue.

"Gee, I can't see anything," Georgia sighed as she wiped ice from the inside of the window. "How are they ever going to finish delivering toys and make it back home in this storm? How can they possibly see?"

An Elf Veterinarian Apprentice 2 (EVA2), standing 3-feet 4-inches tall, with long curly brown hair and big brown eyes, Georgia was recognized far and wide as the reindeer whisperer. An elf with her skills comes along only once in a thousand years.

Known as Gee — not because it was short for Georgia as one might think — but because she had a habit of saying Gee when she spoke.

1

John Eric Johnson

"If only my on-sleigh lighting guidance system had worked," said Georgia's roommate Sasha. "There would be no need for good visibility. Santa would be home by now."

Sasha got the idea of a red light mounted on the front of the sleigh to cut through fog and clouds from her uncle Rudy, who was in charge of making round red foam noses as stocking stuffers. The phrase "if only" was a phrase heard often when talking about a Sasha idea.

Sasha, with short dark hair and a towering height of 3 feet 6 inches, was also an EVA2. She considered herself to be the idea elf of the North Pole. Sasha—who always wore an expression of mischief—was known for her inventions and ideas.

Sometimes her inventions were pure genius and sometimes they were—well—not so genius.

Her rubber booties with traction soles did indeed prevent reindeer from slipping on icy rooftops. But her retractable wings—that would let reindeer glide and save energy—only got in the way and caused the sleigh to crash into a snowbank! No further testing was deemed necessary.

"If only we could spread the reindeer out more to make room for the wings," pondered Sasha. "That would work."

"Can't win 'em all," Santa had said with a smile.

Santa!

Suddenly, Georgia and Sasha heard the sound of sleigh bells! They threw on their blue apprentice uniforms and raced outside to the stables. Fighting through drifting snow and bitter cold they found Santa and eight reindeer covered in ice from head to toe.

Long icicles hung from the antlers while stinging cold breaths formed ice clouds in the frigid night air.

"What happened to the heater and hot-chocolate dispenser?" Sasha asked.

"Stopped working over Cumberland, Rhode Island," Santa answered as he rubbed his hands together for warmth.

Sasha lowered her head.

"Can't win 'em all," Santa said to make Sasha feel better. "They are still two of your best inventions. It was just so cold!"

Santa's face was a light shade of blue and his teeth were chattering so much that Georgia was afraid they would shatter.

Elves scurried about, smothering Santa and the reindeer in warm blankets. Others tripped over each other in their haste to serve hot chocolate to Santa and a mixture of warm barley and honey to the reindeer.

"Ah," Santa said. "Hot chocolate! Hot chocolate is always the right answer!"

Georgia and Sasha draped blankets on Prancer and Cupid and then held them tight, sharing their body heat with the still shivering reindeer. Prancer—who was known to be a bit vain— did not turn away from Georgia's attention, while Cupid just melted into Sasha's embrace.

"Gee, what are we going to do?" Georgia asked Santa in a panic. "This could have been a disaster. We must do something so this never happens again."

Chapter II Changes in the Air

Santa gathered all the veterinarian and reindeer training elves together and called a special meeting for the next morning.

Troy—who taught all the reindeer to fly for as far back as anyone could remember— would be in charge. It was Troy who helped create the original Sensational Six reindeer team—some 300 years ago.

Troy stood exactly 4 feet — tall by elf standards—although he claimed at least an inch more. To stand as straight and tall as possible he firmly gripped his red-and-white-striped cane with his right hand. He chose this cane with Christmas colors because he thought it would make people notice it—instead of his limp.

Elves can sometimes be as vain as humans—although no one seems to care because simply put, elves make toys!

Troy always held a clipboard with pages of neatly written notes. This was how he kept track of the hundreds and hundreds of things he had to—well—keep track of.

His face was a leathery brown from hours in the sun and wind. Combine those features with a beard that looked like a bristle brush and Troy looked much older than his years. To keep everyone on their toes he had a thousand-yard stare that was said to have buckled many an elves' knees with a simple look.

And, if that weren't enough, he always had a piece of black licorice clenched between his teeth and a dribble of black licorice juice rolling down his beard. When he spoke, he didn't open his mouth, for fear the candy would drop out, which caused him to mumble and sometimes difficult to understand.

"It's too much! It's all too much," said Troy. "There are too many children in the world today, which means there are too many toys to deliver. The reindeer team can't handle pulling a sleigh with that many toys. It's just not possible."

"Did he say that there are too many children and too many toys?" asked Georgia. "Can there ever really be too many of either?"

Troy took out his clipboard and started reading from his notes while nervously tapping his cane on the floor.

"The first thing we need to do is something which we have only done once before," mumbled Troy. "We need to add two more reindeer to the team before next Christmas Eve."

There was a loud gasp in the room. Adding two reindeer to the team that had become known as the Elite Eight—in only one year—was pure folly on the part of Troy. Simply impossible!

Troy ignored the crowd's reaction and pushed ahead with his thoughts.

"We will have 20 teams. Each team will consist of two elves assigned to train one reindeer to fly. At the end of the training, the two reindeer with the highest point totals on the final task will join Santa on Christmas Eve next year.

"Here are your assignments. Declan and Cooper, you will be working with Maggie. Kadie and Teaghan will team up with Cameron. Georgia and Sasha will be training Watson."

From that point on Georgia and Sasha didn't hear another word out of Troy's mouth, even though he named 17 more teams.

"Can you believe it—we got Watson," Georgia gleefully said out loud before being shushed by the other teams. More quietly, "Gee, we got Watson!"

"We begin at 7:30 tomorrow morning," said Troy with a menacing look. "And by 7:30 I mean 7 sharp. Do not be late!"

Georgia and Sasha grabbed each other's hands and jumped up and down with joy and excitement. Their eyes as wide as full moons, as they allowed themselves to dream that they could be training the next great reindeer.

John Eric Johnson

Chapter III   Flight Dreams

The ultimate challenge for any elf is to train a reindeer to fly. This specialized training happens so infrequently that there is no definitive training manual to guide them. Or so Georgia and Sasha thought.

It had been 111 years since the Sensational Six was increased to become the Elite Eight. By next Christmas Eve, the team of reindeer would be known as the Terrific Ten. The whole village was abuzz. Biggest thing to happen at the North Pole since the stuffed Teddy Bear—and we all know how big that was.

The night seemed to drag on forever for Georgia and Sasha.

Now the two elves had a firsthand understanding as to what millions of children go through every Christmas Eve waiting for Santa to arrive. Time almost comes to a standstill. In fact, it almost seems to move backward.

At the first light of dawn, Sasha bounded around the room unable to contain her excitement. "Let's go! Let's go, Georgia! We don't want to be late. Come on Georgia let's go!"

"I've been ready for hours," Georgia excitedly said. "Gee, I don't think I slept a wink last night. Let's just get to the stable."

At the stables, Georgia and Sasha found Watson in Stall Number 5. He was just waking up and was a little wobbly on his feet. Of course, Watson always seemed a little wobbly on his feet, as he was always bumping into this and that.

Watson stood five feet tall with legs that appeared to be two sizes too long for his body. It would be impolite to say he was bucked tooth — his mouth was just too small for all his teeth. So small in fact that his two front teeth stuck out—which made him look like he was always smiling. He had large sleepy brown eyes and ears that bent over, unlike all the other reindeer whose ears stood straight up.

Georgia and Sasha looked at each other.

"I think he's perfect—do you think he's perfect?" Sasha asked.

"Absolutely perfect!" Georgia answered.

Precisely at seven Troy walked into the stable and gathered all the training elves and reindeer around him.

"I have some rules and training exercises to go over with you," barked Troy. "Rule Number One: ALWAYS follow the manual exactly as written. The rules were designed for you and your reindeer's safety in mind. Rule Number Two: See Rule Number One.

Troy relished being in charge. He was always spouting gems of wisdom to inspire others, "I can break one candy cane in half with ease. But, put 10 canes together and I can't so much as crack one of them. Work as a team and you cannot be broken."

The training manual was three feet thick—which made it a little shorter than Georgia and Sasha. It encompassed everything about flying from roof landings and takeoffs to wind currents to flying with an unbalanced sleigh.

"So much for there not being a flight manual," lamented Georgia.

Roof landings alone were eight chapters long. It's not enough to just know how to land—reindeer had to be able to land on ice, heavy snow, no snow, shingled roofs, canvas roofs, steep roofs, short roofs, roofs with lots of chimneys and even houses with no roofs.

And, it all had to be mastered before next Christmas Eve.

"But first things first—it's time to learn to fly," smiled Troy as globs of licorice juice ran down his beard. "And understand this— what I say is the law. There isn't a second way to do anything. — only my way. Break any rule and you will be gone from the training faster than you can say Sleigh Bells."

Troy ALWAYS told it the way he saw it. He believed in what he termed Ultra Honesty—which meant he always told the truth—absolutely no exceptions. So what may seem mean and nasty to others was just Troy being Troy.

Georgia thought Troy was being a little harsh with all his rules. After all, flying is supposed to be fun. Flying is supposed to be freedom. What elf wouldn't give their pointy shoes with bells on the end to fly?

Can you imagine? Georgia thought—to be able to fly!

Elves never got to fly because of what came to be known as "the accident".

It happened many years ago when an elf took a reindeer on a rescue flight to save two elves lost in a blizzard. They made it back—but it ended in a terrible crash resulting in injuries to the reindeer and the rescue elf. To this day, that elf walks with a limp.

"And remember." Troy said, while shifting his cane a bit to maintain balance, "there are strict rules against elves flying with the reindeer!"

Troy looked right at Georgia when he said it—as if he knew what she was thinking.

Chapter IV   Leap of Faith

The first thing in the flight manual was for the reindeer to flump ten yards and land—maintain balance and flump again. A flump is half flying and half jumping and is also the sound that reindeer hooves make on rooftop landings. Since an estimated 73% of all takeoffs and landings on Christmas Eve would be in the 10 to 100-yard range—flump training was critical to the success of Santa's sleigh.

However, the most important part of flying and flumping has always been the landing. And everyone knew that the key to a good landing was the two-step stop. This refined method of stopping was developed by an elf named Rusty countless years ago during a particularly harsh winter. Rusty was a student of all things flying and knew that easing into a stop on ice was better than just trying to dig in the hooves and slide. Simply put—it was touch the ground, take two steps, and stop.

"It's all about control," Rusty said often to his young apprentice, Troy.

"Feel the landing," Troy yelled. "Do not fear it. Take two steps and stop."

All the reindeer lined up along a field of snow that was 100 yards long and 50 yards wide. Troy walked the line and draped a silver bell attached to a gold chain around each reindeer's neck.

The bell would continue to ring on flumps and flights for as long as the reindeer remained in the training program. Once the reindeer resigned or was dismissed — the bell would NEVER ring again.

"The best of luck to all of you," said Troy. "And remember the gold is not at the end of the rainbow. The rainbow is the gold."

The first hooves on lesson was that every time Troy blew his whistle the reindeer would flump ten yards and stop. Ten flumps down and ten flumps back.

Tweet!

And all 20 reindeer flumped.

It was like a dance. They all went up in the air and came down ten yards later — just the way Troy designed it.

That is all, except Watson.

Watson was so happy to be given a chance to fly that he put just a tad too much effort into his flump and soared all 100 yards. When he tried to land, he forgot to take two steps and slid into a snowbank and then over the edge of the field and down a steep hill. Watson rolled hooves and antlers end-over-end to the bottom — before crashing to a stop in a different snowbank.

By the time Georgia and Sasha arrived at the end of the field all they could see were four skinny legs and two smiling teeth sticking out of the snow. Then they heard what can only be described as sounds a seal and then a duck would make.

"Aaaagh, quack quack!"

Over and over again.

"Aaaagh, quack quack!"

Georgia and Sasha thought Watson must be hurt until they realized he was laughing.

"Aaaagh, quack quack!"

As they dug him out of the snow — Watson laughed and laughed — and soon Georgia and Sasha were laughing right along with him. And the more they laughed, the harder it became to stop — until all three were rolling on the ground.

"Aaaagh, quack quack! Aaaagh, quack quack!"

Troy, however, was not amused. He glared down from the top of the hill. His face the color of Santa's red suit. His black licorice turned red in his lips. And Georgia swore she saw steam — like you would see over a cup of hot chocolate — coming out of his ears.

"What did I just say?" seethed Troy as he banged his cane in the snow. "Follow the rules. The exercise was to flump ten yards, not 100! Do you want to be one of Santa's reindeer or not? I won't tolerate this! I simply won't tolerate this!"

As hard as they tried, Georgia and Sasha could not stop laughing. They would try to think of something very sad like not having sugar cookies every day, but then they would hear, "Aaaagh, quack quack!" and the laughing would start again.

The rest of the day's training was more of the same. Most of the reindeer struggled to make a 10-yard flump—while Watson struggled to keep from flumping further than ten yards.

Despite a less than stellar first day, Watson, Georgia, and Sasha all headed back to the stables with huge smiles on their faces. Flight training was going to be fun! Not easy, but definitely fun.

"Aaaagh, quack quack!"

After the day's session, Troy met with Santa.

"I've never seen a reindeer make that long of a flump on the first day of training. Twenty yards maybe, but 100 yards is simply amazing. We may have a superstar in our midst. Undisciplined no doubt, but a star nonetheless."

Santa simply ran his hand down his beard and said, "Hmmmmm."

Chapter V Onward and Upward

T he rest of the month was spent increasing the flump distances from 10 yards to 20, to 40, to 80, to 100. While the rest of the reindeer strained to reach those distances, Watson made the flumps with ease.

On the other hand, while all the other reindeer flumped and landed with the two-step method, Watson continued to land at full speed. He would then proceed to slip this way and that way before eventually sliding off the runway into one snowbank after another. A natural in the air — and a natural disaster on the ground.

Despite face full of snow after face full of snow, Watson loved every second of flight training. Even the crashes made him smile. No matter how bad he landed — time after time — his love of being in the air would not be dampened.

As February arrived, reindeer Jamie was dismissed from training. As hard as she tried, she just couldn't keep up with the rigors that would eventually lead to her being able to fly around the world in a single night. Now there were 19 reindeer left.

"No shame in being dismissed, " muttered Troy. "Just remember that just because you put a football in the oven—well that doesn't make it a turkey."

Georgia and Sasha looked at each other and shook their heads side to side.

"Gee that's a new one," said Georgia with a giggle.

Sasha decided that she needed a saying, so she tried out, "Everything is somewhere. Nothing is lost. You just don't know where somewhere is.

"What do you think?"

"I think that saying is nowhere and better off lost," laughed Georgia. "But you keep trying. You can't win 'em all."

Chapter VI   Time to Solo

February's training would focus on flying—leave the ground, circle the field and land. Sounds simple enough but, as most would soon learn—flumping 100 yards was definitely not flying.

"Believe in yourselves," said Troy. "That's the key to being a good flier. See yourself doing it and you will do it. You gotta believe."

Georgia and Sasha knew Watson could fly, but there was no way they could have predicted what was about to happen on his maiden solo flight.

First to solo was Eddie. He took off and circled the field and landed with ease.

"Whew," thought Tracie and LJ, his elf trainers.

The biggest fear was that a reindeer would gain some altitude, look down, and lose confidence in his or her ability to fly and forget everything they had learned. Not the end of the world, but a nose plant always leaves a funny dent in the snow.

Next up was Maggie. She had been a star in the flumping part of training, so it was expected that she would excel at flying. With a flawless solo flight, she left little doubt as to who was a frontrunner to join Santa's team.

Maggie effortlessly circled the field and landed so softly that it appeared she hadn't even squashed a snowflake.

Thelonious, Zevon, and Jackson were not so lucky—as they all seemed to forget their training as soon as their hooves left the ground. Thelonious and Zevon circled the field with the control exhibited by a leaf on a windy day. They were just lucky and very happy to be back on the ground.

Jackson started fine but was so nervous on his landing that he forgot the two-step maneuver and landed snout first— sliding 20 yards to a stop. Ouch!

All three asked to be dismissed from training by day's end. Flying wasn't for the faint of heart.

Then it was Watson's turn. Georgia and Sasha hugged Watson and told him to just do only what was asked—circle the field and land. Just be himself and he would do great. In hindsight, this turned out to be terrible advice.

"Gee, you got this Watson," said Georgia. "You were born to fly. Just breathe and believe."

With a smile on his face from ear to ear—Watson took a running start and took to the air and started to circle the field. But he was having so much fun that he forgot about doing what he was instructed to do—circle the field and land.

He became so lost in the moment that he shot straight up for one mile waving his hooves awkwardly and laughing "Aaaagh, quack quack!" as he went.

Then he tucked his legs under him and sped back down towards the village and practice area.

"Aaaagh, quack quack!"

He pulled out of his dive just over the head of Troy who had dropped his cane and was limping away as fast as he could. As Watson whizzed over Troy's head, he accidentally knocked Troy's stocking cap off. Oh, oh — not good!

Georgia and Sasha waved their arms and yelled for Watson to land, but he was just getting started. In the blink of an eye, he had flown out of sight to the left, and then before Georgia could say, "Candy cane," he had passed over the field and disappeared in the other direction.

"Gee, look at him go," exclaimed Georgia. "There has never been such a flier."

"Watson you need to land," screamed Sasha. "You need to get back on the ground."

Troy was less enthusiastic about Watson's flying skills as he threw his clipboard and spit his licorice on the ground. Nobody knocked his hat off!

"I'm in charge here," Troy shouted as he kicked his hat. "Land immediately!"

After a couple more high-speed passes — which included one where Watson was flying upside down — he came in for what can only be described as more of a crash than a landing.

John Eric Johnson

Going too fast and not even attempting a two-step landing, Watson misjudged the ground, stubbed his left hoof, and did a nose plant that had him bouncing down the runway like a rubber ball. And each time he bounced up, the sound of "Aaaagh, quack quack!" could be heard.

Georgia, with hands-on each side of her face, watched in horror at the bouncing reindeer. Sasha just covered her eyes and hoped that she would wake up from what had to be a nightmare.

Troy turned to Santa and said, "Never in all my years have I seen such disregard for the rules. But never have I seen a better exhibition of flying. Watson is light years ahead of any reindeer as a flier, but light years behind when it comes to landing.

"I should dismiss him from the program for that stunt but…"

Ninety-nine times out of a hundred, Watson crashed on landing. Most of the time it was a spectacular failure with him rolling end over end — aaaaghing and quacking until he stopped.

Santa looked at the mound of snow that was now Watson, ran his hand down his beard, and said, "Hmmmmm."

Chapter VII   Soft Landings

Immediately after Watson's solo Georgia and Sasha were called into Troy's office.

"You need to get control of your reindeer," Troy fumed. "If he doesn't hurt himself, he is going to hurt one of the other reindeer or one of us. If you can't control Watson, I'm going to have to wash him out of the program. Are we clear?"

The words "wash him out of the program" echoed through Georgia and Sasha's thoughts over and over again.

"Gee, he is the best flier of any reindeer including any of the Elite Eight," said Georgia.

"But he is a danger to everyone including himself on his landings," sighed Sasha as idea after idea ran through her head. "If he can't land in snow how is he ever going to be able to land on a roof? It's up to us to help him. Or it will be up to us to mend his broken heart."

Sasha quickly went over to the room where all the stuffed toys were built and took wheelbarrow after wheelbarrow of goose down stuffing and spread it five feet high on the runway. Georgia gathered four sensors similar to those found on remote control racing cars that beep when the cars get too close to a wall or piece of furniture. It was time to get creative!

Once on the runway, Georgia, attached the sensors to Watson's hooves so that the alarms would flash and beep just before he touched down. It was a genius idea that had less than genius results. "If only!"

On his first landing, Watson glided slowly over the stuffing and when he was just inches above it the lights and buzzers started flashing just as the elves had planned. But try as hard as he could, Watson just couldn't quite get the timing correct and he tumbled into the stuffing with an "Aaaagh, quack quack!"

Again and again, they tried landing after landing, and, each time, Watson was just a little late with his two-step technique and gently crashed into the stuffing.

Although crash after crash came and went, Watson never got discouraged. He never thought of quitting. All he wanted to do was fly. And he was flying. He was living his dream and there was no better feeling in the world.

"Aaaagh, quack quack!"

Watson's love of flying aside, if he couldn't land safely then he couldn't be trusted pulling Santa's sleigh. One small misstep on a roof and it could be disaster for all the reindeer and Santa. If he wanted to be chosen, he had to learn to land perfectly — not just now and then but — every single time.

Chapter VIII Heartbreak

May was considered the make-it or break-it month. Every roof and every landing had to be handled perfectly to remain in flight training.

"Gee he can't even land in toy stuffing without crashing," sighed Georgia. "How on earth is he ever going to handle this? I fear for him."

"I fear for all of us, but I have another idea," winked Sasha.

She took out her famous anti-skid boots—and attached them to Watson's hooves. Watson took a few awkward steps, stumbled a bit, and then off he went!

The first roof was nice and flat, but Watson came in too fast and despite his anti-skid boots slid right off the end.

"Aaaagh, quack quack!"

The next roof was very short, and Watson missed the roof completely and went headfirst into another snowbank.

"Aaaagh, quack quack!"

Then came a roof that was so steep that the area in which to land was only 13 inches wide at the peak. This was Watson's best effort, but he stubbed his right hoof at the last instant, slid down the side of the roof, went up in the air, and splat into yet another snowbank.

"Aaaagh, quack quack!"

This went on day after day. Watson tried and tried and tried. And then tried some more. Watson, Georgia, and Sasha stayed late every day and continued to work on the landings even after all the other reindeer had retired to the stables and a nice warm meal.

On the last day of the month, Troy, with clipboard in hand, motioned for Georgia, Sasha, and Watson to join him near the flat roof. Moving his licorice from one side of his mouth to the other, he mumbled what Georgia and Sasha feared the most, "I'm sorry but I have no choice but to dismiss Watson from the flying program. He just doesn't have what it takes. He is the best flier I have ever seen, but he is just too dangerous to be a part of a team. Watson's out."

As Watson listened to the words, he felt as if his heart had left his chest and become lodged in his throat making it difficult to breathe. His eyes filled with tears as his head and shoulders slumped forward. His lower lip quivered as Georgia reached over to wipe away a single large tear rolling down his cheek.

Sasha wrapped her arms around his neck and hugged him with all her might. It was the saddest day anyone could remember at the happiest place on Earth.

The other reindeer watched as Watson, Georgia, and Sasha walked the length of the runway and disappeared into the stable and Stall Number 5. Watson's bell fell silent.

John Eric Johnson

It was the first time anyone could ever remember Watson not smiling and laughing. It was the first time anyone had seen three hearts break as one.

Chapter IX   New Dreams

The following morning, Georgia and Sasha showed up at Watson's stall just as the other reindeer were leaving for their training session. Watson stood with head down staring at the floor. His dream had ended.

Georgia brought his favorite snack, a grain-covered apple with a carrot in the middle. Sasha arrived with a knitted hat she decorated with tiny snowmen on it to keep his ears warm—but Watson could not be cheered up.

Could there ever be anything better than flying the Christmas Eve sleigh?

And could there be a worse feeling than to be a flier who was grounded? Grounded with no chance of redemption.

Watson could think of none as despair and hopelessness grabbed hold and refused to let go.

"Gee, Watson, let's get you out into the sunshine and fresh air," said Georgia fighting bravely not to cry. "Come on buddy it's not the end of the world."

But for Watson it was.

As the days turned to weeks and then months, the reindeer training continued with some success and some failure. While

Maggie and Finn excelled, Meg, Ella, Marcus, Taraska, Cameron, and Annabelle were dismissed.

Troy was starting to doubt his claim that he could train two new reindeer well enough to join the Elite Eight in only one year. He felt only Maggie would be good enough by Christmas Eve.

Meanwhile, life had gone on for Watson, Georgia, and Sasha. The trio remained as close as ever—even without the daily rigors of flight training.

And every now and then—when no one was looking—Watson took to the skies and just flew and flew. He could go up or down, left or right, and sometimes even backward if he had a strong headwind. He just couldn't land without getting a face full of snow. For him, the freedom he found in flying was worth every second and every snowflake up his nose.

"Aaaagh, quack quack."

Then on one late summer day—as they walked out of the stable—Watson turned and bumped into a heavy wooden door with a thud. Georgia and Sasha had seen Watson bump into something a thousand times before, but this time they had seen something as clear as the noses on their faces. And it made them very happy.

With Watson chasing after them, Georgia and Sasha raced down to the training area.

"Excuse me, but this area is open only to trainees working to become part of Santa's reindeer team," barked Troy who was beginning to crack ever so slightly under the pressure he had put on himself. "You no longer belong here. Go away!"

Santa, standing near, looked up and put his hand on Troy's shoulder.

Troy nodded.

"Kindness is better," Santa whispered under his breath.

Georgia walked over to Santa and asked him to bend down. When he did, Georgia whisked his glasses off of his nose. Santa stood abruptly and grabbed his chin as if he were in deep thought. Georgia then spun around and placed the glasses on Watson's nose as a bewildered Santa looked on.

Sasha made a slight adjustment and whispered, "Believe in yourself and show them who you are. This is not the time to hold anything back. Make an impression, just not with your face in the snow," she winked.

With that, Watson burst straight up and out of sight. At the top of the climb, he turned and raced back down towards the training area. This seemed like a rerun of his first solo.

Legs bent back and tucked under his body he was hitting speeds no reindeer had ever come close to. The force of the dive pushed his wide-open eyes back in his head as tears rolled off his cheeks. A spider web of bulging red blood vessels formed in his eyes. He struggled to focus.

Watson was going so fast his two front teeth chattered. The vibration and airflow ripped past his body as he struggled to keep his legs tucked underneath him. Air was driven through his mouth and into his lungs making it difficult to breathe as he hurtled closer and closer to the ground.

"Everyone get out of the way," screamed Troy. "Watson is going to crash! RUN!"

Georgia and Sasha stood their ground. They had asked Watson to believe in himself and now they needed to show they believed in him too. But just to be on the safe side they had their eyes closed tightly. Just in case.

The space between Watson and the ground quickly melted away. Now just inches above the snow he made an amazing turn. His belly slightly grazing the ground as he sped towards Troy. This *was* déjà vu.

Troy ducked and prepared for an out of control 400-pound reindeer to crash into him. His life actually passed before his eyes —at least that's what he said afterward—as he waited for the imminent impact.

However, Watson had other ideas on how to make a lasting impression. As he flew over Troy, Watson reached down with his mouth and gently lifted Troy's hat off his head.

"He knocked my hat off again," stammered Troy as his body shook violently. "He did it again!"

It was a superb exhibition of flying which meant it was now time for a perfect ending. Watson made a quick circle in the sky — and came all the way around and landed with a textbook two-step stop — so that his nose gently pressed up against Troy's. Watson smiled, he bowed and placed Troy's hat back on his head.

"Aaaagh, quack quack!"

"Gee we knew it. We knew it," Georgia said to Santa "I don't know how we missed it."

"It's the glasses," exclaimed Sasha, bursting in laughter.

"He couldn't land before because he couldn't see the ground clearly. Watson needs glasses."

Santa ran his hand down his beard and said, "Hmmmmmm!"

Georgia and Sasha ran to Watson, throwing their arms around him while jumping up and down screaming "Aaaagh, quack quack!" over and over again.

Santa took in this joyous dance in the snow and just nodded in Troy's direction. Troy, however, missed the signal as he was still trembling from what almost happened.

"I," stammered Troy as he struggled to catch his breath. "I think..."

It was time to get Watson back in the air. And it was time for Watson to celebrate. And that meant fresh carrots, and, on this special occasion, a candy apple covered in oats. It was also time for Watson to smile again!

Chapter X Believing is Seeing

While Santa's glasses were a quick fix for the demonstration, they wouldn't do for flying around the world. Watson needed reindeer glasses, and there was only one elf up to making this one-of-a-kind item—the idea elf—Sasha.

They had to be tight to Watson's head with no chance of falling off. Watson losing his sight while flying Santa's sleigh would be disastrous. So, while Santa wore small round spectacles, Watson needed very large glasses with straps to hold them in place. Sasha decided on building goggles with one strap going around his head and one strap going under his chin. The lenses bubbled out, so Watson had a panoramic view of his surroundings.

Sasha worked on the goggles from sunrise to sunrise before she had a pair that met her high standards. If she did say so herself— and she usually did—they were spectacular.

The moment of truth had arrived when all her hard work and Watson's dreams would be put to the test. It was time for Watson to get an invite back to the tryouts or go home for good. There was no third option, nor would he ever get another chance if he failed on this day.

Fingers crossed, Watson, Georgia, and Sasha walked to the training area. The sun was shining brightly, and the sky was a deep sapphire blue absent of any clouds.

A slight breeze from the south raised newly fallen snow into the air forming a glistening white wall of ice crystals for the trio to walk through. For those watching from a distance, it looked as if the threesome had magically appeared out of thin air.

Georgia removed her gold St. Nicholas medal from around her neck and attached it to Watson's bell. She hoped the medal would clang on the bell as he flew making the sound they all longed to hear again — the bell ringing.

Sasha meticulously attached Watson's goggles, making sure that each strap was tight and the lenses were in the proper position and clean. She kissed Watson on his forehead for good luck and took a deep breath in. The idea elf closed her eyes tight and wished as hard as she could that Watson would soar like an eagle and land as soft as a snowflake.

As Watson slowly walked to the starting point, he kept his head held high and his focus on the job at hand. Troy drew and X in the snow with his red and white striped cane to designate the spot where Watson had to complete his landing. If the landing were off by so much as an inch Watson would be dismissed.

Georgia was so nervous that she watched through a break in her fingers as she covered her eyes with her hands. Sasha—eyes still tightly shut—reached over and put her arm around Georgia.

As the flight drew closer—more and more reindeer and elves gathered—until all residents of Santa's Village were in attendance. Like, two combatants, Troy and Watson stood inches apart and stared into each other's eyes. Both refused to blink.

"I do hope you know how much I want you to succeed today," Troy whispered in a surprisingly gentle voice. "How much we all want you to succeed."

Watson broke his stare just long enough to nod.

Troy commanded Watson to take to the air. Watson glanced over to Georgia and Sasha, took a short hop, and lifted off from the ground. The tension that filled the air was as thick as a Mrs. Claus fudge brownie. Not as tasty but certainly as thick.

"Aaaagh, quack quack!"

John Eric Johnson

Watson gained altitude and began circling and turning to his left at every corner of the field. This time there were no aerobatics or high-speed passes. On this flight, Watson was doing only what he was told to do to the letter. Of course, that didn't mean he wasn't having fun.

"Aaaagh, quack quack! Aaaagh, quack quack!"

The crowd watching was so quiet that a pin dropped in the snow would have made a thunderous sound. Hands were wrung and hearts were beating faster as Watson turned onto short final approach. This was the moment of truth.

"Come on you got this Watson," whispered Georgia. "Just a little more and you got this."

The flight was picture perfect right out of the flight manual until just before he landed. Suddenly a strong gust of wind caused snow to rise from the ground making it impossible to see the landing area. The crowd gasped in anguish knowing full well that if Watson couldn't see the ground that a now-famous Watson face plant was about to be showcased.

As the snow slowly cleared and the crowd could see again there was Watson smiling from ear to ear as he stood on the X in the snow. There was no stumble or any kind of bumble. Watson was perfect and the crowd erupted in tumultuous cheers.

"Aaaagh, quack quack!"

Sasha threw her hands in the air and smiled a smile as wide as Watson's, as Georgia danced and spun around in circles. All the

42

other reindeer, including the Elite Eight, smiled and pounded their hooves on the snow in approval. It was such a glorious moment that even the stoic Troy found himself clapping and laughing along with everyone else.

Not quite out of the woods and back on the list of potentials just yet, Watson still had to prove himself on roof landings. And, as if he had been doing it all his life he proceeded to land on a flat roof, a steep roof, a house with no roof, and even a boat. He succeeded at every task Troy asked of him. And Troy asked a lot from Watson. No, he asked more than a lot. He asked for perfection.

Watson rose to the occasion on every task. And, as a ruby red sunset backlit a line of Christmas trees with a red glow — Watson was a flier again!

"Many times what appears to be the end of the road is just a place to turn around and begin again," spouted Troy.

As Santa nodded and pulled on his beard with a "Hmmmm," Troy exclaimed that Watson needed to be at practice the following day. He had a lot of ground to make up if he was going to be a part of the team.

With the announcement that Watson was back in the running to pull Santa's sleigh, he jumped straight up and at the top of his jump a very faint "Aaaagh, quack quack" could be heard along with the ringing of a tiny bell. Then all anyone on the ground could see was a light tan streak shooting across the sky.

"Aaaagh, quack quack! Aaaagh, quack quack!"

Chapter XI   Time to Shine

The following day, Watson, with Georgia and Sasha in tow, resumed his training. There were crosswind landings, night flights, flights in storms, and long-distance endurance flights. And Watson excelled at them all.

As summer quickly turned to fall, four more reindeer, Harriet, Eddie, Gael, and Rose, were either dismissed from training or resigned. Now there were only six left of the original 20.

It was now time to start flying as a team. First, it would be two reindeer flying together, then four, then six, and finally flights with the Elite Eight. These six had proven themselves worthy of an opportunity to show their stuff with the eight best flying reindeer in the world.

At first, Watson found it difficult to fly with other reindeer. He was such a strong and gifted flier that the other reindeer just couldn't keep up. He had to learn to fly at the weakest reindeer's pace. The goal as always was to fly to protect Santa, the sleigh of toys, and of course the other reindeer.

As the weeks went by, it looked like Watson and Maggie were the favorites to join Santa's team. They had both proved to be excellent fliers under all conditions. Watson was faster but Maggie was quicker. Watson was stronger but Maggie had more endurance. No lasting advantage to either in a contest that was sure to remain undecided until the last day.

Georgia and Sasha were also feeling quite good about Watson's chances at this point.

"I would bet 12 sugar cookies that Watson will make the team," said Georgia to Sasha.

"Why don't we just forget the bet and just eat the cookies," smiled Sasha.

By November, and with only seven weeks until Christmas, it was time for the remaining six reindeer to be teamed up with the Elite Eight of Dasher, Dancer, Prancer, Vixen, Comet, Cupid, Donner, and Blitzen. These eight reindeer were the best of the best, so if Watson and Maggie wanted to fly with them, they had better elevate their flight game from very very good to excellent.

First, it was Maggie and Finn who flew with the Eight. Finn was a very smooth and effortless flier, but he lacked the strength of the others — which left Maggie and the rest of the team straining to pull the sleigh.

Then it was Watson and Rory. Rory had proved himself to be a powerful flier, but his power would trip him up on the two-step landing. Rory often needed an extra step to stop and, while that was fine when he was flying alone, it was a real problem when flying with nine other reindeer.

Watson himself was certainly not perfect in a team of ten. He, like Rory, did his best flying by himself. He loved being free in the air, but in a team of ten, he needed to be just that — part of a team. It took him several weeks to adjust and a lot of patience by the Elite Eight, but, when Watson finally got the timing and speeds correct it was as if he had been doing it his whole life.

It would all come down to the final flight test, which was a night flight three days before Christmas. There would be stops in areas all around the globe. The route featured frigid weather in the mountains and heat so high in the desert it would blister the red paint on the sleigh.

And, as luck would have it there was a powerful blizzard tracking towards Rhode Island in the USA. What better way to end an exhausting around the world flight than to fly into a raging snowstorm before returning to the North Pole? At least that's what Troy thought.

And, just in case the blizzard wasn't enough of a challenge for the team, Troy had selected Klepper Bluff for the final roof landing. Klepper Bluff was located 15 miles off the coast of Rhode Island on tiny Block Island. The house on Klepper Bluff was built on a finger of land that jutted out high above the Atlantic Ocean. Three sides of the house extended to the edges of the finger — which provided spectacular views in every direction.

John Eric Johnson

What made this location such a difficult obstacle were the dangers involved. First, the landing point was a house perched on a three-sided cliff. Second, the winds were notoriously fickle, gusting and shifting. Third, there were the rocks that lined the bottom of the bluff at low tide and crashing waves with hidden rocks underneath at high tide.

Troy selected this as the final landing site because it was a maker or breaker of confidence.

Unfazed by any of this and still in the running to make the Terrific Ten were Rory, Maggie, Finn, Watson, Asil, and the smallest reindeer of all, Hallie.

What Hallie lacked in size, she made up ten times in heart. Hallie loved to be told she couldn't do something. As soon as she heard those words of negativity, she knew in her heart she would succeed. No drama, it was just done.

Asil was the Zen reindeer. On paper, she would appear the weakest of the twenty-original reindeer, but here she was still battling for a spot. Asil worked harder and spent more time practicing than any of the others. While some thought she was just burning holes in the sky — which is a nice way of saying she was just wasting her time — she was learning all aspects of flying. At this point, she considered herself one with the sky, thus the Zen.

The sleigh was loaded with heavy crates to simulate what it would be like pulling Santa's sleigh. And Troy would be the driver — with one coach from each team allowed to ride along.

Georgia and Sasha used the tradition of breaking a wishbone to determine who would ride with Troy. A large ten-inch wishbone was found to be perfect for the challenge.

Each elf took an end. Georgia took hold right at the very bottom of her side. Sasha on the other hand gripped her end much higher. Then they agreed to switch sides since each thought the other had a better more resilient side of the wishbone. Then they switched back and then back again. They switched so many times they each lost track of where they originally started.

"Good luck Sasha, smiled Georgia as she put slight tension on her end.

"Same to you Gee," said Sasha. "Let the chips of this wishbone fall where they may."

There are two schools of thought on winning at wishbone. One is to pull slowly and deliberately and the other is to pull with a quick jerk of the hand. However, neither is a guarantee of a win.

Georgia and Sasha both started slowly, and both tried to remain serious. But the more they pulled the more they giggled until snap. Pieces of dried wishbone flew in all directions while the two largest pieces remained between the thumbs and forefingers of the two elves.

"Too close to call," said Troy looking at the two pieces. He measured it this way and that and still couldn't tell.

It wasn't until the idea elf herself came up with a brilliant solution to determine the winner.

"We will stand the pieces on end and shine a bright light behind them," smiled Sasha. "Then 30 feet away we will put up a white sheet. The illuminated wishbone pieces will be enlarged on the screen allowing us to easily determine a winner."

So a light was set up and a screen installed and lo and behold she was right. They looked and looked and measured and measured some more until it was finally determined that the winner by the width of a doll's fake eyelash was Georgia. Her dream of flying was about to come true.

"Congratulations Gee!" said Sasha. "Promise me you'll tell me all about the flight. I want to hear every detail. I'm so envious."

Georgia felt happy and a little sad at the same time. After all, Sasha was her best friend and Sasha wanted to be on the flight as much as she did.

"Gee Sasha it really was too close to call," said Georgia. "We should just do it over."

"Absolutely not," said Sasha. "You won fair and square. I do not have an if only here."

With that Troy pulled Sasha by the arm to a distance where Georgia couldn't hear their conversation.

"Fair and square," spewed Troy. What a bunch of bad eggnog.!"

"Bad Eggnog," countered Sasha?

"You adjusted the lighting ever so slightly so it appeared that Georgia had won when I could clearly see that you were the winner," steamed Troy pointing a finger in Sasha's face. "You won!"

"Shhhhhh," whispered Sasha.

"Why would you give up on a once in a lifetime ride in Santa's sleigh," asked a more subdued Troy.

"Because it's not my dream," said Sasha. "It's Georgia's, so please don't tell her. Promise me you won't EVER tell her!"

"Hmmmmm," stuttered Troy. "Not a word unless I'm asked. I will not lie."

"Besides I'm afraid of heights," said Sasha with a wink as she walked away.

Maggie's coaches, Deklan and Cooper, decided to have a gumdrop-eating contest to determine a winner and a ride on Santa's Sleigh. Whichever elf could put the most gumdrops in their mouth and then eat them the fastest would be the winner. In only one minute both elves jammed 43 gumdrops into their cavernous mouths. Their cheeks looked like balloons just before they popped from too much air. How they could chew is still a mystery. But chew and chew and chew they did.

With eyes bulging and teeth churning away Cooper won as he swallowed the last of the 43 gumdrops just seconds before Declan finished. The problem was that after finishing off that many candies in just a matter of minutes neither elf was feeling particularly well. One might even say they both looked as green as the mint gumdrops they just ate.

Troy took one look at them in disgust and decided neither was fit to make the flight. As he announced his decision, he swore he saw both elves smile at each other, wink and breathe a sigh of relief. As he had said earlier, flying isn't for the faint of heart.

The four other teams decided they would pass on the flight as well. A number of excuses were used such as, "My winter coat is at the cleaners", and "I really want to go but I think I get airsick and so on." Yes, flying wasn't for the faint of heart.

"Okay listen up," commanded Troy. "Names were drawn out of a stocking to determine the teams and order of flights. The first to take off will be Asil and Hallie. Remember, your number one priority is safety. Good luck to all and to all happy landings."

The final challenge would be judged on teamwork, landings, strength, endurance, and general flying. Each category will be scored on a 1-10 scale. The two reindeer with the highest scores will join the Terrific Ten. In case of a tie, Troy will determine which reindeer will make the team.

No reindeer had ever scored a perfect 50 and none was expected to record a perfect score on this stormy night either.

Asil and Hallie lucked out on their flight having made their stop at Klepper Bluff just ahead of the storm approaching from the south. The winds were relatively calm and there was only a dusting of snow on the rooftop. The flight was as easy as it gets.

Not a surprise to anyone, Asil and Hallie scored well during their three-hour flight. Asil scored higher on landings and strength, and Hallie was better at teamwork and general flying. Asil scored 41 and Hallie 42.

After a short break and a flight review by Troy, it was time for Rory and Finn to showcase their long-distance flying skills. Rory seemed a bit on the nervous side as he scratched at the snow with his left hoof. He appeared less than enthusiastic about making this flight. Finn, on the other hand, was already in his flight harness chomping at the bit to get going.

Best friends since they were just calves, Rory and Finn flew in perfect harmony with each other. When one stumbled a bit the other was there to pick him up.

The biggest challenge became the worsening storm conditions off the coast of Block Island. The snow was accumulating at three inches per hour while sustained winds of 25 knots with gusts topping out at 40 were recorded.

Both had trouble seeing and then landing in windy and icy conditions. They simply lacked experience. However, both scored a 43. They were now the frontrunners.

As the weather continued to deteriorate the question became go or no go on the final flight. If this were Christmas Eve the answer is very simple — GO. But, is the risk too high on a training run? What if something happens to the sleigh or worst yet the reindeer or riders?

Opinions differed but the final decision was a go. Troy was assigned the task of landing on Klepper Bluff or selecting an alternate location if he determined Block Island too dangerous. The word on fliers is that good decisions come out of making bad decisions and Troy was about to make a very very bad decision.

The time was at hand for Watson and Maggie. Watson's heart was thumping so hard that when Georgia rested her hand on his chest, she could feel it beating under her fingers. Sasha tightened and wiped his goggles and gave him a kiss on his nose for good luck.

"Aaaagh, quack! quack!"

Maggie was ready to go as all the other reindeer slammed their hooves in the snow. It was their time to shine.

Georgia climbed into the sleigh and took her seat on the right-hand side of Troy. She immediately grabbed onto the sleigh railing in front of her.

"Nervous?" asked Troy. "Nothing to be nervous about."

"Except falling out of the sleigh at a very high height," thought Georgia to herself. "Maybe it's not too late for Sasha to take my place."

Georgia spotted a smiling Sasha off to the side giving her a thumbs up for luck. Georgia half-heartedly returned the gesture.

"I'll be right here waiting with a hot chocolate for you," yelled Sasha. "Your dream of a lifetime is about to come true."

Georgia thought, "A dream and a nightmare are still both dreams, aren't they?"

There was a slight jerk as the sleigh began to move forward. Slowly at first and then faster and faster down the runway. Georgia looked over the side and watched as the sleigh lifted off the ground and the shadow beneath became smaller and smaller.

"I'm flying," Georgia said with a giggle. "I'm actually flying. Wait, I'm flying?"

The sleigh rose at a steep angle pushing Troy and Georgia back in their seats. As Santa's Village disappeared from below the reindeer and sleigh entered a thick layer of puffy white clouds. With nothing but white all around, Georgia became disoriented. Up was down. Left was right.

The moisture in the cloud soaked her face and clothes. Her hands were now clamped onto the underside of her seat and she could swear her fingernails were digging indentations into the wood.

It was so quiet and peaceful that Georgia was startled when the sleigh broke through the top side of the clouds. What she saw before her was breathtaking for as far as her eyes could see.

The sky was the clearest she had ever seen. All around her were thousands and thousands of bright diamonds poking holes in a black tapestry. The stars seemed so close she thought she might actually be able to grab one and put it in her pocket.

The clouds below appeared like a river made of cotton candy. Her hands loosened their grip as she soaked in a world she could only have imagined before this very moment.

"Ahhhhh," sighed Georgia. "Is this real?"

Troy simply looked over and smiled.

The first location on this journey was a steep snow-covered roof in the French Alps. Watson kept thinking that if he just stayed at the pace of the other reindeer that he would be okay. The first landing and takeoff were perfect.

Watson exhaled a sigh of relief. "Whew!"

Then it was on to a house with a grass roof in Dublin, Ireland. Landing on a grass roof meant a gentle stop—otherwise, the reindeer and sleigh could burst through the roof. Again perfection.

There was a tent in the outback of Australia, a mud roof in South Africa, a tin roof in Mexico, and a shale roof in Japan. All were completed perfectly. And after each landing and takeoff what could be heard was "Aaaagh, quack quack!"

Watson's laugh and joy were so genuine that the other reindeer started laughing and Aaaaghing and quacking right alone with him. Maybe they had forgotten how special it was to be chosen to pull Santa's sleigh. Maybe they forgot that this was supposed to be a joyous occasion. And maybe Watson was there to remind them.

The final test of the night was Klepper Bluff. The conditions had worsened significantly since the first two test runs. The winds were gusting so strongly that limbs were breaking off of trees and flying by the sleigh in flight. And visibility had been reduced to a hand in front of Troy's face.

Not even the Elite Eight had ever flown in such bad weather. One wrong move and disaster could strike. It had become so dangerous that Troy was thinking of bypassing Klepper Bluff and heading to the alternate landing spot. Unfortunately, his ego got the better of him and he decided to stay on course and land.

The first sign of trouble came when Watson's glasses started to ice up. At first, he could see a little and very quickly he couldn't see at all. And, to make matters worse he had no way to signal the other reindeer or Troy that he was in distress.

For only the second time in his life, his smile disappeared from his face as he desperately turned his head side-to-side, trying to get a glimpse of something, anything. Maggie was the first to realize Watson was struggling but she too had no way to signal Troy.

Watson frantically waved his legs in hopes that one of the other reindeer would see him and abort the landing.

"I think Watson is in trouble," shouted Georgia as the sleigh was being violently bounced about like a cork on the ocean. "Troy, we need to…".

The wind gusts forced the team to make constant speed adjustments to stay airborne. As they approached the roof, a tailwind snuck up on them causing their airspeed to increase. They were flying too fast to land and they had no way of knowing it.

Watson, who was all but blind, was flying by feel alone. He stumbled as soon as his hooves touched the snow-covered roof.

While the other reindeer did their best to stop, Watson was out of control, sliding first this way and then that way across the roof. His momentum was so strong that he slid into Maggie, knocking her off of her feet. She strained to dig her hooves in to regain control, but it was too late as both slid off the peak of the roof.

John Eric Johnson

It took all the experience and skill of the Elite Eight to bring the sleigh to a halt. The force of this sudden stop jerked Watson and Maggie back slamming them into the side of the house with a loud thud. They dangled over the edge of the roof unable to free themselves.

No longer lined up on the roof, the reindeer lost control of Santa's sleigh as it slowly turned sideways. The sleigh, with Troy and Georgia aboard, started to slide down the roof. Slowly at first, then picking up speed until it was just inches from sliding off into the ocean and onto rocks below.

The reindeer struggled to stay on their feet as the weight of the sleigh pulled them closer and closer to the edge. This was as dangerous a situation as the Elite Eight had ever experienced.

As the sleigh tilted and slid violently, Troy and Georgia tumbled over the side railing. Only Troy's quick thinking—hooking his cane to the railing—kept him from falling into the ocean. He reached for Georgia's hand as she fell past him, but she slipped through his grip, and onto the rocks below.

"No no no," screamed a distraught Troy. "Nooooooo! "

Before he could regain his composure and get back to the emergency at hand, he felt a slight tug on his right shoe. When he looked down, he found a desperate. Georgia clinging to a single bell on the toe of his shoe.

"Hang on, Georgia," yelled Troy. "Hang on."

Troy tried to work his way up the icy cane, but his hands slipped again and again until he was holding onto just the rubber knob on the bottom. Georgia was holding on with everything she had, but she too was losing her grip.

Troy knew if he didn't react immediately all would be lost. The reindeer, the sleigh, he and Georgia and any chance Santa had of delivering toys on Christmas Eve would all fall into the ocean.

Troy shouted, "On three, all reindeer jump straight up."

As the sleigh continued to slide Troy yelled, "Forget counting. Jump straight up! NOW!!!!!"

The reindeer jumped as high and as fast as they could. Straining and snorting with all their might they were slowly — inch by inch — able to drag Santa's sleigh back up onto the edge of the roof.

As soon as Troy regained his footing he reached down, and with all his remaining strength pulled Georgia to safety. Then as the sleigh begins to rise in the air they climbed aboard and held onto whatever they could grab.

Legs flailing and eyes closed under the strain, the exhausted reindeer pulled and pulled to free Maggie and then Watson who was by now hanging upside down. Watson's goggles were caught on the edge of the roof until the straps finally broke and the goggles fell into the ocean far below with a splash.

Troy barked out commands which could barely be heard over the howling winds, "All reindeer move forward — then up, up, up."

To lighten the sleigh's load, Troy slowly and ever so carefully worked his way over to the release lever and freed the massive crates loaded in the back. The crates slid over the side and fell, shattering into a thousand pieces on the rocks.

Georgia's shaking hands were still tightly locked around the bell on Troy's shoe — which was no longer on his foot. She tried to talk, but no words came out.

Once Troy felt that the sleigh and reindeer were aligned again, he gave the command to fly straight ahead and then straight up as fast as they could go.

"Go go go," Troy commanded

It didn't take the reindeer long to fly clear of the blizzard and set a heading for home. There was no more laughing. There was no more joy. There was only relief that the reindeer and sleigh had survived.

Chapter XII   Goodbye Watson

As the sleigh neared the North Pole, Troy told Georgia the very last thing in the world she wanted to hear. She was going to have to climb over the team of reindeer in flight and cut Watson loose from his harness.

Troy couldn't afford to try to land and have Watson trip again and do damage to the team or sleigh. Watson had to be set free for the good of the team. For the good of Christmas.

"Gee, no! Please no!" cried Georgia. "I don't want to leave the sleigh. I don't want to go out there. I can't. I just can't. What if I fall?"

"It's the only way Gee," said Troy with a soothing tone in his voice.

"What will he do by himself?" said Georgia still shaking from the near disaster at Klepper Bluff. "I'll talk him down. I'll hold onto his neck and talk him down."

"He's lost his goggles," Troy said sadly. "He can't see well enough to land! It would be too dangerous for the other reindeer! But he can make it back by himself. You will cut him loose and he will fly home on his own. It's the only way. There is too much at risk. There are only two days until Christmas."

John Eric Johnson

With tears streaming down her cheeks and hands shaking out of fear, Georgia began the dangerous climb out to Watson. She looked at the distance between her and Watson as well as the distance between her and the ground. One seemed impossible to cover while the other... well, she didn't want to think about the other.

Georgia leaned as far forward as she could and grabbed hold of Dancer's tail. She took a deep breath and leaped onto Dancer's back. From there she slowly worked her way up to Dancer's neck, head, and then snout.

Another deep breath and another leap until she was able to grab hold of Comet's tail. She climbed over Comet and then Cupid and finally Dasher. With each move, Georgia held on as if her life depended on it — because it did.

By the time she was able to grab Watson's tail and jump onto his back 40 minutes had gone by. Exhausted, cold, and scared to her core she moved hand over hand, over his back until she was hugging Watson around the neck.

"I love you, Watson. I love you, Watson," she cried as she squeezed him tighter and tighter. "It wasn't your fault. It was my fault for not thinking the glasses through better. It's all my fault."

Georgia explained to Watson what was going to happen, although she felt as if he already knew. She would undo his harness, and, when she gave Troy the signal, the team of reindeer would turn hard to the left, leaving Watson flying all by himself.

Once that happened, he should follow the sleigh back to the North Pole and land the best he could.

Georgia hugged him one last time and climbed up as far as she could so that she could look him right in his eyes. "I love you, Watson!"

She then reached out and undid his harness and climbed over the middle support so that she was now on Maggie's back. With a mighty tug and the raising of her hand, the team of reindeer turned hard to the left leaving Watson alone in the night sky.

"Watson follow us," she screamed. "This way. Watson, please! Please follow us."

Watson stayed straight on his flight path and Georgia watched him until he faded from sight. Georgia sobbed uncontrollably as she pushed her face into Maggie's neck.

"Watson! Watson! Watson!"

"Hold on Georgia," shouted Troy knowing there was no way Georgia was going to be able to make it back to the safety of the sleigh. "Stay where you are and hold on."

The team of nine reindeer made it back to the North Pole and landed with ease. Several of the trainer elves worked together to pry Georgia's hands from Maggie's mane. Her brown eyes, red from crying, searched the sky for any sign of Watson. But Watson was gone.

Chapter XIII   Follow Your Heart

The sun was still tucked behind the horizon the following morning as Georgia and Sasha raced up the snow-covered road to Stall Number 5. He had to be there. He simply had to be there. But as they turned the corner the sadness in the other elves' eyes and the bowed heads of the other reindeer told them otherwise. Even before they arrived at Watson's empty stall, they knew he wouldn't be there.

"We have to go find him. Come on, Sasha, he has to be out there somewhere", said Georgia frantically.

"I can't go with you I'm on a special top-secret assignment for Santa," said Sasha as tears streamed down her cheeks. "I can't go."

"Doing what?" snapped Georgia her patience drained. "What is more important than finding Watson? Everyone, let's go! Watson needs our help."

But no one moved. It was two days until Christmas and no elves or reindeer could be spared for the search.

Sasha looked up. Her eyes filled with tears.

"I'm so sorry Gee," said Sasha. "We are all sorry."

Georgia sat helplessly in the straw and cried into her hands. She felt alone.

Santa walked over to her, bent down, wiped away her tears, and simply said, "Follow your heart, Georgia. You can never go wrong if you follow your heart."

"I don't know what to do," sighed Georgia. I don't know where to look. My heart is broken. How do I follow a broken heart?"

"Be silent and listen and the answer to your question will come," smiled Santa.

Georgia sat and pondered Santa's advice before responding, "Rule number one Santa is find Watson and bring him home safely."

"What's rule number two," asked Santa?

"See rule number one," smiled Georgia.

With that, she jumped to her feet and raced through the stable where she grabbed a blanket, two snowshoes, two snow paddles, and some grain. She hurriedly threw them into a backpack and ran out into the snow.

"Okay heart where would you like me to go?" asked Georgia. "Don't be shy. Speak up."

Georgia headed west since that was the direction she last saw Watson flying. The snowshoes kept her from sinking down into the deep snow and the snow paddles on her hands allowed her to push herself back up onto her feet every time she fell. The snow paddles were another brilliant idea of Sasha's—if she did say so herself.

She trudged through the snow for several hours breaking new trails as she walked. Snow flurries quickly turned into a light snowstorm. A deep to the bone chill had grabbed hold of her and wouldn't let go.

Georgia was so cold she could no longer feel her fingers or toes, and her nose looked like a giant icicle attached to her face. She was covered from head to toe in snow and

felt like any one of the hundred snowmen she had once built at Santa's Village.

For just a moment Georgia imagined how nice it would be to be sitting by a crackling fire with a warm mug of hot chocolate piled high with whipped cream. There was of course a plate of fresh-baked sugar cookies within easy reach. Her toes so warm she'd have to take her boots and socks off. How wonderful that would be!

She quickly shook her head and returned to the reality of being miles away from the Village cold and lost. Reality sometimes stinks she thought.

As she plodded on, it began snowing harder and harder making it more difficult to walk. To make matters worse the wind was whipping by her at an alarming rate forcing her to lean into it to keep from being blown over.

Georgia was faced with the toughest decision of her life. To make it back to Santa's Village she would have to turn around now. She couldn't take even one more step. But that meant giving up on Watson.

"What do I do?" said Georgia as ice formed on her cheek where a tear was frozen in its' tracks. "What was it Santa said? Follow my heart."

Georgia stood perfectly still and closed her eyes and thought about what she really wanted. What was her real heart's desire? Was it a warm fire and hot chocolate or was it finding Watson?

She opened her eyes and spotted a lone pine tree bent over from the wind just over the next ridge. "That's where Watson is," she thought. "That's where I would be if I were lost."

Was that her heart speaking to her or was it just the cold leading her down another icy path to nowhere?

As she came across the top of the hill, she spotted what appeared to be a light tan figure sitting slumped over at the base of the tree. Could it be? Could it be Watson?

"Watson," Georgia yelled. "Watson!"

The tiny figure with its head drooped forward almost to the ground turned to look at her. Its' face was covered in ice. There was no way to tell where the ice ended and the body began.

She ran down the hill as fast as her tiny legs would carry her. However, because her legs were so short, they never cleared the top layer of snow resulting in stumbles and falls again and again. Each time she fell she got a fresh face full of snow. First, she lost her hat then one snowshoe and then the other, but she refused to stop moving.

As she drew nearer, Georgia could see Watson sitting in the snow violently shaking. His face was grey, and his eyes were half-closed. Icicles hung from his snout and antlers. Every painful breath he took shot streams of ice-cold air out his nostrils.

"Watson! Watson!" Georgia screamed.

As she flung her arms around him and hugged him tightly, she could feel his cold body through her jacket.

"Watson, it's me Georgia," she cried. "Watson!"

Quickly, Georgia pulled a blanket out of her backpack, wrapped it around Watson, and turned on the battery pack. It was the same type of heated blanket that Santa used on his Christmas Eve flights. Another Sasha invention to the rescue.

Even though she was shivering right along with Watson, she tore off her jacket and wrapped it around Watson's head and rubbed his ears to warm them.

"Watson look at me," said Georgia as snow began to build upon her face. Her eyelashes were ice, and her ears were burning from the cold.

"Watson, are you okay? Are you hurt?" stammered Georgia as she dug through the snow with her bare hands to check him for any injuries.

Georgia fully realized the dire situation they faced. In a short period of time neither would be able to move. Hypothermia would set in as too much of their body heat was lost. If they reached that point, they would no longer be able to function. It became now or never.

"We have got to get out of here. You have got to get us out of here. I can't walk anymore. I've lost my snowshoes. You have to fly us out of here. Watson, do you hear me? You have to fly us out of here."

72

Watson looked down at the building snow and gently shook his head side to side. He just couldn't do it. He couldn't even stand he was so cold. Besides, he wasn't a flier anymore.

Georgia grabbed Watson by his antlers in an attempt to get him to understand that time was running out and he needed to fly. He was a flier and he needed to fly.

NOW!

"Come on, Watson, this is it," cried Georgia. "You've got to try. I know you can do it. Please, get on your feet and try! Stand up!"

Turning to look at Georgia, Watson attempted to smile but his lips were frozen shut. It took all the strength he had, but he slowly and painfully stood. The warm blanket was helping to clear the ice from his body, but would it be enough?

"That a boy, Watson. I believe in you. I always have. Get on your feet.," said Georgia.

Georgia removed the coat from Watson's face and took the blanket and wrapped it around herself.

As quickly as she dusted an inch of snow off Watson, two more replaced it. She climbed onto Watson's back and grabbed onto his mane and squeezed her fingers as tight as she could.

The snow was too deep for a running takeoff, so Watson would have to jump straight up if he were going to fly. Watson strained to look over his shoulder to make sure Georgia was holding on tight. He bent his knees, took a deep breath, and jumped, and fought his way into the air.

Rising an inch at a time, he struggled against the wind and the cold. Especially, the cold which left him drained and on the verge of unwillingly giving up.

Watson's back was slippery with ice and snow. Georgia started to slide off to the left, but Watson was able to turn his body sideways to the right so that she could climb back on. Once settled, Watson started rising through the storm. Snow slammed into his face stinging him like a swarm of bees. He squinted to save his eyes from the searing pain, which made it nearly impossible to see.

Georgia had lowered her body as close to Watson's back as she could. She needed to stay out of the oncoming snow. Snow buildup on her would eventually become so heavy that Watson would sink back to the ground.

"Come on, Watson, you're doing great," encouraged Georgia.

After a brutal 30 minutes in the air, Georgia could finally make out the lights at Santa's Village.

Georgia breathed a loud sigh of relief before she realized a crash landing was coming.

"Okay Watson we made it too far to fail now," said Georgia into his ear. "Let's finish this dance."

Watson looked back at Georgia and gave a wry smile. It was time to land. She was about to experience a Watson face plant firsthand.

On the ground, elves ran towards the runway. Some carried blankets and some had hot chocolate and hot barley with honey.

Watson was trying to think of how to land with Georgia on his back and not hurt her. If ever he had a perfect landing in him, now was the time to break it out.

"Don't worry about me Watson," Georgia shivered. "Focus on your landing. Believe in yourself."

His eyes stung from the relentless oncoming snow. His body was stiff from the cold. And Watson was just plain out of energy. Whether he wanted to or not, he was coming back down to earth. He looked back at Georgia one last time. She gave him a small smile and a thumbs up.

He turned back just in time for his hooves to hit the snow. As he attempted the two-step landing, he stumbled forward, caught his balance, stumbled again, and collapsed to his knees. From there he slid 20 yards before coming to a stop—in yet another snowbank.

Quickly he shook himself free and looked back to see Georgia, but she wasn't there. He turned his head from side to side as he frantically scanned the area for her. And then total relief overwhelmed him. Not three feet to his right were two elf shoes with bells on the toes sticking out of a nearby snowbank.

"Aaaagh, quack! quack!"

John Eric Johnson

Three elves with shovels and a portable heater rushed to Georgia's aid and quickly dug her out. Once free she sought out Watson immediately. She found him off to her left with his smile still intact. Most beautiful thing I've ever seen she thought.

"You did it, Watson," sighed Georgia as she ran to him and threw her arms around his neck. "You did it."

Both were quickly surrounded by 30 elves, who wrapped them in warm blankets and carried them to the stables.

It didn't take long for both to warm up as they drank their fill of hot chocolate and hot barley and honey. Georgia kept her arm draped around Watson the entire time and Watson ran his cheek across Georgia's every chance he had.

That night Georgia slept in Stall Number 5 with a heated blanket over her and Watson.

In another part of the stable Santa and Troy were discussing what had gone wrong on the training flight and believe it or not what had gone right.

"I'm sorry Santa," moaned Troy. "I almost ruined Christmas for millions of children around the world. And I almost destroyed the sleigh, your sleigh, as well as the reindeer team, myself and Georgia."

"Effective immediately I'm done," said Troy with a sadness that Santa had seldom seen before. "I hereby resign."

Santa stared directly into Troy's eyes for a long uncomfortable moment.

"Yes, there almost was a tragedy," said Santa as he wiped his glasses. "But—and here is the reality of this situation—almost doesn't count. Nothing was ruined and, in the end, all was saved.

"There is no question that you made a bad decision to fly to Klepper Bluff," smiled Santa. "Then when things went a little—let's say haywire—okay a lot haywire—you stood tall and made every decision correctly. Because of your actions, none of the almosts ever happened.

"Now you can quit if you want," Santa said as he placed his hand on Troy's shoulder. "Or you can accept not being perfect like the rest of us and continue in the position which seemed to have picked you so many years ago. Stay or go. Your choice."

Troy shook his head and with a tear in his eye said, "I'll sleep on it, but under the circumstances, I don't believe I should be at tomorrow's ceremony to announce the winners."

"Under the circumstances, I must insist you be there," scolded Santa. "Without you, there would be no Terrific Ten, so you will be there even if I have to put you in a toy sack and carry you there myself. Are we clear?"

"Clear as your glasses," smiled Troy.

Chapter XIV $CS

Georgia opened her eyes—on the day before Christmas—and smiled as a sleeping Watson snored and moved his legs as if he were running. Her smile was short-lived, however. Reality will do that.

This was the morning that the two new members of Santa's reindeer team would be announced. Watson's blunder on his test flight surely eliminated him from contention. Georgia's heart was breaking as she thought of his disappointment.

Watson also knew what to expect at the presentation. But he was a flier, and no one could ever take that away from him. Oh, how he loved to fly! As much as it hurt, he would stand there with head and antlers held high and stamp his hooves in the snow in approval of the two winners.

Elves and reindeer alike gathered just outside the Village entrance in anticipation of the historic announcement. After a long year of making toys, in preparation for Christmas Eve, this was a time for celebration and congratulations.

Tables were piled high with every imaginable cookie, muffin, pie, brownie, and cake. The smell alone was a thing of beauty and probably added a few pounds to everyone attending.

And, then there were tables upon tables of hot chocolate, hot cider, candies, fruits, and grain-covered apples filled with carrots.

A hush came over the crowd as Troy and Santa made their way to the stage

Georgia, who had her arm draped over Watson, noticed that Sasha stood beside Santa. In her right hand, she carried a silver box.

"What is Sasha doing up there," Georgia said to Watson. "And what's in that box?"

"Attention! Attention," Troy shouted while tapping his cane loudly on the wooden floor. "ATTENTION!

"As most of you know there was a heroic rescue last night by two of our very own," said Troy. "First, Georgia, EVA 2, went out alone and on foot in search of her friend and reindeer in training, Watson. And, once she found him it was Watson's turn to be a hero and fly them both to safety. For their efforts, they are both being awarded the Silver Christmas Star!"

The SCS, as it was called, was the highest award any elf or reindeer could receive and had been awarded only one other time.

Georgia and Watson approached Santa who placed the Stars attached to candy-cane-colored ribbons around their necks. They beamed and Georgia waved as cheers and stomping hooves filled the village with the sweet sound of admiration. It was the first time since the accident—on the roof—that Watson's smile shown bright again.

As Georgia and Watson left the stage Troy returned to the podium.

"And now it's time to announce the two reindeer who will join the Elite Eight, who from this day forward will be known as the Terrific Ten. After 12 months of grueling flight training, we have determined these reindeer to be most worthy of joining the best of the best."

Troy looked down at his clipboard and said, "The first and highest point scorer at 45 is Maggie. An excellent flier and strong teammate—she will be a wonderful addition to the team."

Maggie dipped her head in appreciation as elves cheered and reindeer stomped their hooves in approval.

Now the area grew so quiet a whisper could be heard all the way on the other side of the Village.

Santa walked to the podium, "For the second reindeer we have a three-way tie between Rory, Finn, and Watson."

Watson, the crowd uttered in unison. Wasn't he out of contention for his blunder on the final test flight?

Watson and Georgia turned to look at each other in amazement.

"Gee you're still in the running," Georgia exclaimed to Watson. "I don't think I can stand the suspense anymore."

"And, as you know all ties are decided by our very own reindeer wrangler, Troy," Smiled Santa.

With that Troy walked back to the podium.

"What's going on," Georgia mouthed to Sasha?

"Shhhh, it's a surprise," smiled Sasha.

Troy cleared his throat and placed his clipboard stacked with papers on the podium. His eyes looked down as he proceeded to read a long dissertation as to the strengths of each of the three reindeer. There was no such list of any weaknesses. The crowd hung on his every word as they patiently waited for the announcement.

Sasha smiled ever so slightly as she stepped off the stage to be with Watson and Georgia. Gee was so nervous that she grabbed Sasha's hand so tightly that Sasha winced in pain.

"Ouch", moaned Sasha. "Breaking my fingers isn't going to change the final outcome," she smiled.

"Sorry," grinned Georgia sheepishly. "It's just until this very moment I didn't think there was any way…"

Troy looked up and scanned the crowd without actually making any eye contact. His face was etched with the anguish of someone about to give very bad news instead of one announcing very good news.

"Come on Troy get on with it," someone in the crowd yelled. "I've eaten so many cookies that I've gained 15 pounds."

The crowd roared in laughter, which seemed to ease some of the growing tension.

"Sometimes just believing isn't enough," said Troy. "Sometimes you need a little help in getting your dreams to come true. This is one of those times."

Troy walked to Sasha and took the silver box.

"Yesterday Santa asked our idea elf, Sasha, to work her magic," said Troy as he opened the box to reveal what appeared to be some sort of new-fangled flying goggles. "So, out of her imagination, she came up with these special goggles that are heated so they will not ice-up in the cold and cooled so they will not fog up in the heat. They have extra heavy-duty straps so they will never fall or be torn off. And they will allow our other new addition to the Terrific Ten to be able to see and fly the way he was meant to fly."

Watson, with eyes opened as big as oatmeal cookies, slowly looked at Georgia whose hands covered her mouth in disbelief.

"It is with great pleasure and complete confidence that we announce the newest member to the Terrific Ten—Watson," exclaimed Troy with a seldom-seen smile!

Sasha gave Watson a big hug and a kiss right on his snout as Georgia hugged him with all her might.

The elves cheered and the reindeer stomped their hooves in celebration. Confetti rained down from the Elite Eight who were circling above.

"Congratulations, Watson," Santa smiled. "And congratulations Georgia and Sasha for making a dream come true." Santa then leaned in and whispered, "For all of us."

As the celebration ended and she was walking back to the stables—Georgia glanced back at Troy. For an instant, she swore she saw a piece of a glimmering SCS medal hanging around his neck on a candy-cane-colored ribbon. When she looked again, he was gone.

Chapter XV   Merry Christmas

As the sun began to set elves scurried and hurried to load the sleigh with what can only be described as a mountain of toys. Hours and hours and hours of elf power and hard work by all culminated in this joyous moment.

Songs were sung. Hot chocolate was drunk. And, of course, cookies were gobbled down.

Watson and Maggie were nervously taking their spots with the other members of the Terrific Ten. Even with all the specialized training and hours of flying, they realized there is nothing that can prepare a reindeer for its' first Christmas Eve flight.

Georgia and Sasha were there to affix Watson's goggles and to wish all the reindeer a safe and speedy trip.

"We will be here with food and warm blankets when you return," said Georgia as she tickled Watson's right ear.

"And remember that if you just believe in yourself half as much as we believe in you then we believe in you twice as much as you do," laughed Sasha. "I thought I'd beat Troy to the silly line of the day."

As they walked back towards the sleigh Georgia and Sasha overheard Santa comment to Troy that it may be time to cut back on the mountain of toys given away. The sleigh was overflowing with toys and even with the Terrific Ten, this was going to be a very long and difficult night.

"We will talk when I return," said Santa. "Put on your thinking cap."

"I will be here," smiled Troy with a nod.

"But fewer toys," gasped Troy. "That would be like drinking only half a cup of hot chocolate or eating only half a sugar cookie. Who would ever do that? Fewer toys will just not do."

Santa grabbed hold of the sleigh's railing and climbed into his customary center seat. He jokingly asked Georgia if she would like to fly along, which she quickly declined.

"I've eaten too many gumdrops and my wishbone is too short and I left my winter parka back in the village…," she laughed. "I think it will be a very long time before my feet leave the ground again. A very very very long time."

Just as Santa was about to give the command to fly, Watson turned back to Georgia and Sasha. His eyes were filled with happy tears as he flashed a brilliant two-tooth smile, bowed his head in appreciation and winked. He was sure to light up the night sky.

"Aaaagh, quack quack! Aaaagh, quack quack!" bellowed all ten reindeer.

Santa took the reins and raised his voice to the sky: "On Dasher, on Dancer, on Prancer and Vixen, on Comet and Cupid, on Donner and Blitzen."

After a slight pause and another smile, Santa yelled, "On Maggie, on Watson dash away all!"

As the reindeer and sleigh rose in the sky and streaked off to make Christmas wishes come true for children all around the world, Sasha leaned over to Georgia and whispered, "I have a brilliant idea. We will shrink the toys before they go on the sleigh and then make them full size when Santa delivers them. That way he can deliver even more toys. What do you think?"

Georgia glanced at Sasha and while running her hand down her chin simply said, "Hmmmmm…"

Acknowledgments

I would like to thank Bernard Mendillo, Robert J. Hawkins, Joe Broadmeadow, Isabel Arribas (for the amazing illustrations,) and Lizbeth Reilly for their assistance and patience in bringing this story to print.

I would also like to thank Tink for her unending ideas and Asil for teaching me to follow my heart.

About the Author

John Eric Johnson grew up in Cumberland, Rhode. He earned a degree in journalism from Utah State University. Throughout his writing career, he worked in various fields including newspapers, magazines, public relations, advertising, and business communications.

"Watson And the Terrific Ten" is his first book. It will not be his last!

About JEBWizard Publishing

JEBWizard Publishing offers a hybrid approach to publishing. By taking a vested interest in the success of your book, we put our reputation on the line to create and market a quality publication. We offer a customized solution based on your individual project needs.

Our catalog of authors spans the spectrum of fiction, non-fiction, Young Adult, True Crime, Self-help, and Children's books.

Contact us for submission guidelines at

https://www.jebwizardpublishing.com

Infor@jebwizardpublishing.com

Or in writing at

JEBWizard Publishing

37 Park Forest Rd.

Cranston, RI 02920

CPSIA information can be obtained
at www.ICGtesting.com
Printed in the USA
BVHW011140031220
594824BV00025B/253